To Mr. Patterson.
The best school shows ever.

SIMON & SCHUSTER BOOKS FOR YOUNG READERS
An imprint of Simon & Schuster Children's Publishing Division
1230 Avenue of the Americas, New York, New York 10020
Copyright © 2013 by Rebecca Patterson
First published in 2013 in Great Britain by Macmillan Children's Books.
First US edition 2014

The text for this book is set in Celestia Antiqua Std.
The illustrations are rendered in mixed media and digital.
Manufactured in China
0714 MCM
2 4 6 8 10 9 7 5 3 1
CIP data for this book is available from the Library of Congress.
ISBN 978-1-4814-0114-2
ISBN 978-1-4814-0115-9 (eBook)

. . . because my Granny says
I was the BEST THING in it!

But I don't care . . .

After the show the Angel says SOME
people should NOT be in shows AT ALL!

I forget to go off,

and the
Important Angel
has to WAIT!

Then I sing in the right part, but
dance the WRONG WAY!

I sing in the
WRONG PART!

And the show begins.

I think it's going well, until . . .

We all go
onstage—
quietly, with no
pushing please!

EVERYONE is here!

It's almost time for our show! The Baby Jesus is ready,

the Angel has brushed her hair,

and one of the recorders has a tummyache.

Remember
No SHOW + TELL on Thursday

The Angel came down and said

We miss show-and-tell
so we can get ready.

And now it's Thursday. The Big Day!

We practice all afternoon.
It takes a long time!

But then Miss Bright gives me a dish towel for my head and tells me I'm a shepherd!

I'm not even in the
Donkey Dance!

So in this show I
think I am almost . . .

nothing.

I'm not the
Important Angel,

or a King.

I'm meant to sing a little,

but when did we all learn THIS song?

I know I'm not
a narrator,

or a recorder.

Ashton and
Claudia are
the BIG parts,

and Connor
is the triangle.

I wasn't listening when
Miss Bright gave out
the parts,

so I don't know
what I am.

We are putting on a Christmas Show!

Rebecca Patterson

The CHRISTMAS SHOW

Simon & Schuster Books for Young Readers

New York   London   Toronto   Sydney   New Delhi